A SPRING TREASURY
of Recipes, Crafts, and Wisdom

ANGELA FERRARO-FANNING & ANNELIESDRAWS

HEY, this book was a **REALLY GOOD CHOICE!**

Not just because it's a **GREAT BOOK** (of course we'd say that), but because it is **PRINTED ON RECYCLED PAPER** made from 100% post-consumer waste. Turning a tree into new paper uses a lot of energy, water, and chemicals. But turning waste paper into fresh paper again uses a lot less of those resources.

Did you know that most picture books are made in countries on the other side of the world, so they travel a long way to get here? This special book was printed right here in the US, so the **CARBON FOOTPRINT FROM SHIPPING IS LOWER**, too.

This more **PLANET-FRIENDLY** way of making books costs more, so why did we bother? Because at Ivy Kids we know that our young readers will inherit the world we create today, and we think those children want a **HEALTHY, HAPPY PLANET**. (As well as awesome books to read).

WE HOPE YOU ENJOY IT!

IVY KIDS

iVY KiDS

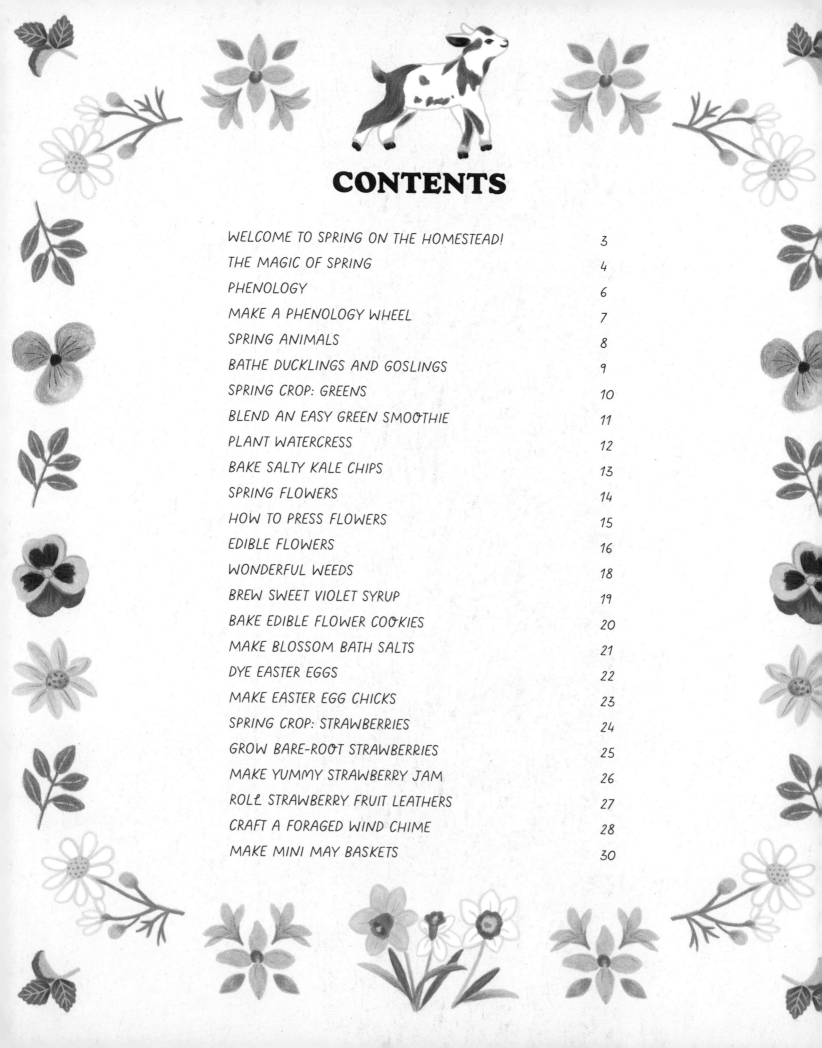

CONTENTS

WELCOME TO SPRING ON THE HOMESTEAD!

Spring is one of the busiest seasons. It's a time for new life and new beginnings. All around, nature is hard at work—and so are we!

Crops such as kale, watercress, and strawberries can be planted, then harvested and enjoyed later in the season. Edible wildflowers can be foraged and used to make sweet syrup and tasty cookies.

There are spring holidays to celebrate with homemade gifts and seasonal recipes, and it's a perfect time for outdoor adventures and craft projects that use natural materials.

This season offers an abundance of fun and opportunity.

Turn the pages and see how you can join in!

THE MAGIC OF SPRING

In the spring, nature comes to life again. Animals wake up from their winter sleep, baby lambs and kids are born, and ducklings and chicks are hatching. The earth thaws, flowers emerge and bloom, the days grow longer and warmer, and we can finally spend more time outside. Discover some of the things you can do and experience during this special season…

BUGS, such as spiders and beetles, begin to emerge

FRESH FLOWERS can be foraged and pressed for homemade cards

BABY ANIMALS are born

4

NEW LEAVES bud on the trees

Greens, such as **SPINACH**, can be planted early in the season

We can use natural dye to decorate eggs for **EASTER**

STRAWBERRIES are ready to pick late in the season

When the crocus blooms in spring, it's time to plant "cool weather crops," such as lettuce, peas, and radish.

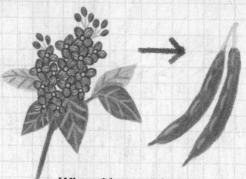

When lilacs and apple trees blossom, plant cucumber, green beans, and squash.

If iris and peonies bloom, it's warm enough to plant peppers, eggplant, and melon.

When peach and plum trees blossom, it's a good time to sow carrot, beet, broccoli, radish, cauliflower, and cabbage seeds.

PHENOLOGY

Phenology is the science of reading nature's signs and discovering the relationships between plants, animals, and insects. Natural events, such as the opening of flowers, can help farmers and gardeners to plan for the arrival of certain insects and to know when to start planting crops. We can even look at plants and their behavior to predict weather, such as rainfall! Here are some common springtime examples ...

Can you spot tulips or daffodils closing their petals? If so, rain is on the way! The plants do this to protect their pollen from rainfall.

Lily of the valley blooms signal the time to plant tomatoes.

Watch for morning glories to blossom—this means Japanese beetles will arrive soon!

Watch for dandelions to open—this means it's time to plant potatoes.

MAKE A PHENOLOGY WHEEL

Do you think there are relationships between plants, animals, or weather in your own backyard or local park? You can make a phenology wheel to keep track of what's happening in nature around you.

YOU WILL NEED:

- A LARGE SHEET OF PAPER OR A PAPER PLATE
- SOMETHING CIRCULAR TO TRACE, SUCH AS A PLATE
- SCISSORS
- A RULER
- A PENCIL
- MARKERS OR CRAYONS

1 If using paper, trace a large circle in the middle of the sheet of paper, then carefully cut the circle out. If using a plate, skip to step 2.

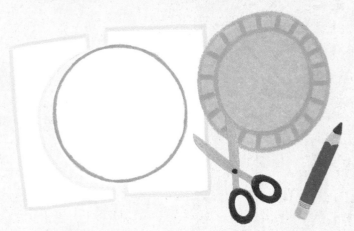

2 Use a pencil and ruler to divide the circle/plate into sections. Create as many as you like.

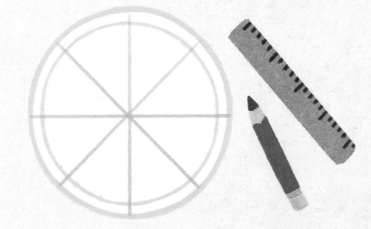

3 Use each section to record a relationship you see in nature. Start by choosing one section and write down or draw what you see. For example, which flowers are blooming? Which insects are arriving? Do the flowers react to the weather?

4 Continue watching nature throughout the spring and keep drawing and writing down the relationships you notice!

5 After you've completed your phenology wheel, be sure to keep it as a reminder for what to expect next spring!

SPRING ANIMALS

Spring is such an exciting time on the homestead because new barnyard family members are arriving! Baby birds hatch from their eggshells and goat and sheep mamas are busy tending to their new babies. All baby farm animals have their own special food and need different care. A farmer's job is to help the hatchlings, goat kids, and lambs grow to be healthy and strong after they're born.

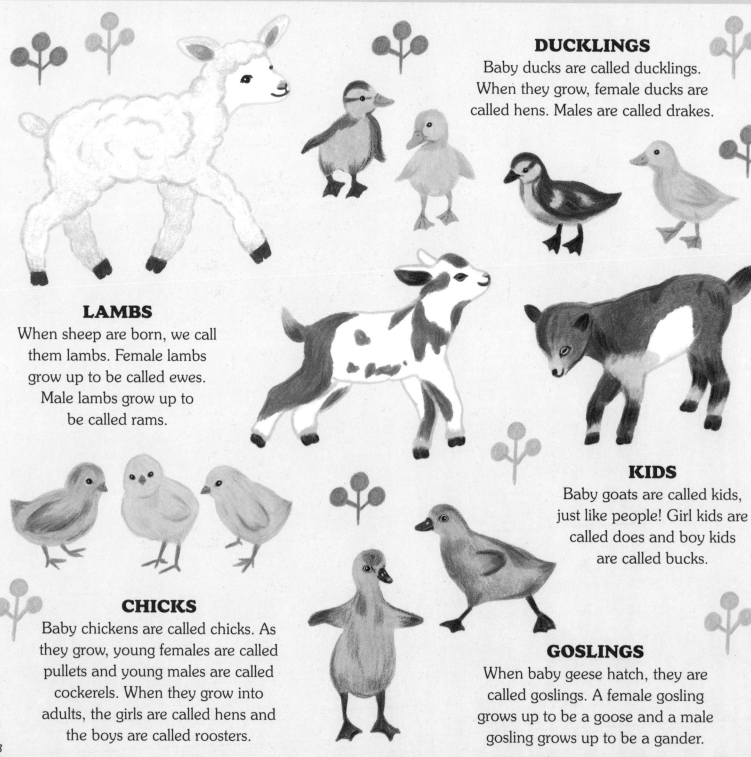

DUCKLINGS
Baby ducks are called ducklings. When they grow, female ducks are called hens. Males are called drakes.

LAMBS
When sheep are born, we call them lambs. Female lambs grow up to be called ewes. Male lambs grow up to be called rams.

KIDS
Baby goats are called kids, just like people! Girl kids are called does and boy kids are called bucks.

CHICKS
Baby chickens are called chicks. As they grow, young females are called pullets and young males are called cockerels. When they grow into adults, the girls are called hens and the boys are called roosters.

GOSLINGS
When baby geese hatch, they are called goslings. A female gosling grows up to be a goose and a male gosling grows up to be a gander.

BATHE DUCKLINGS AND GOSLINGS

Ducklings and goslings love to play in the water. They have so much fun swimming, cleaning themselves, and preening. Once their grown-up feathers develop (at about six weeks old), they can swim as much as they like, but until then, these baby birds need a helping hand! This is because the fuzz they are born with doesn't dry easily. Read the steps below to find out how to safely bathe them.

1 Fill a shallow bucket, container, or sink with room temperature water about 2 inches deep. Make sure it's not too hot nor too cold.

2 Carefully help the ducklings and goslings into the water one at a time. They will immediately start splashing and playing!

3 After about 5 minutes, it's time to remove the birds for their safety. Carefully remove each duckling or gosling and place it on a bath towel.

4 Very gently, wrap the towel around the bird's body (never the face and beak) and help them to dry off. Do not squeeze or rub the bird, because this can cause injury.

5 Replace the ducklings and goslings back into their brooder box under their heat source so they stay warm as they dry.

TIP: DUCKLINGS AND GOSLINGS LOVE TO EAT SMALL BITS OF LETTUCE OR DANDELION FLOATING IN THEIR BATH WATER! MAKE SURE THE PIECES ARE SMALL ENOUGH SO THAT THEY DON'T CHOKE.

FACT: CHICKS AND CHICKENS DON'T LIKE TO BATHE IN WATER. THEY PREFER TO ROLL IN DIRT INSTEAD, WHICH IS CALLED A DUST BATH!

TIP: BABY BIRDS SHOULD BE AT LEAST 48 HOURS OLD BEFORE SWIMMING.

ROMAINE LETTUCE

This crisp and crunchy green is a popular lettuce choice since it grows well all spring and summer long. Available in green and red colors.

RADICCHIO

A red or purple leaf often shaped like a cabbage. This is a bitter-tasting leaf that's used mostly in salads. It's thick and crunchy.

KALE

Kale can be bitter and tough to chew when raw. If massaged with oil or dressing, or cooked, it's quite delicious! Kale can be curly or wrinkled, purple or green.

SPRING CROP: GREENS

Some crops thrive in the cooler temperatures and wet weather of spring. Most greens are sensitive to the strong summer sun, dry days, and excess heat. They have shallow root systems so are happiest when grown in partial shade with plenty of moisture in the soil. Let's look at different colors and flavors of spring greens.

ARUGULA

This peppery tasting green is somewhat spicy and is delicious in salads and sandwiches. When arugula gets too hot in late spring, it bolts and sends up a shoot with a white flower on the end. This flower is edible, white, and shaped like a star!

SWISS CHARD

Chard comes in many different color varieties such as red, yellow, pink, white, and orange! The leaves are large and can be difficult to chew. These greens are delicious when cooked.

SPINACH

Spinach is full of vitamins and protein. It's great for making smoothies, eating in salads, and is tasty when cooked. Some spinach leaves are wrinkly and some are oval-shaped.

BLEND AN EASY GREEN SMOOTHIE

Greens grow very quickly in the spring and can be ready to harvest in as little as 35 days after planting seeds! With so many green varieties maturing all at once, it can be difficult to use them before they wilt. But greens aren't just for eating in salads! We can combine tasty leaves with fruit in a blender to create a delicious and healthy smoothie.

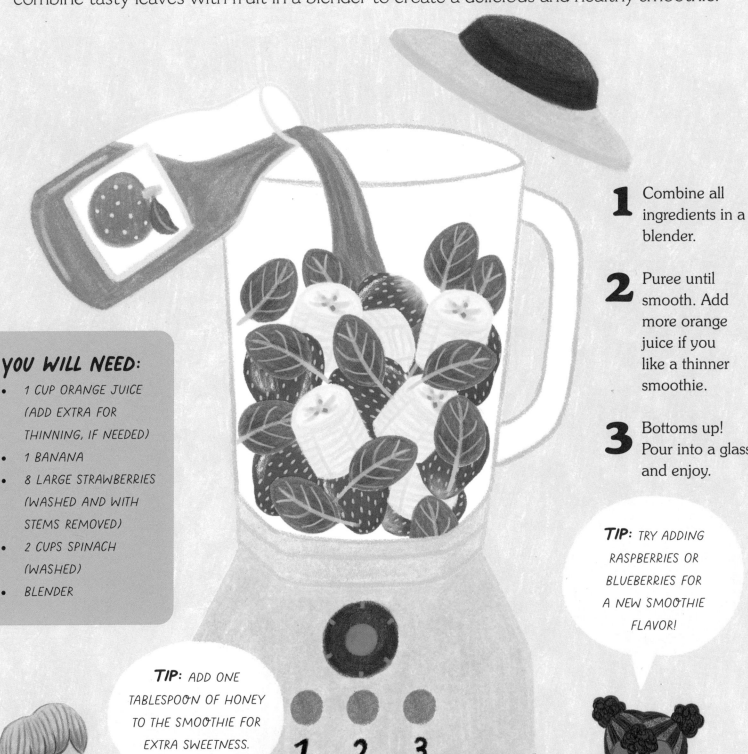

YOU WILL NEED:
* 1 CUP ORANGE JUICE (ADD EXTRA FOR THINNING, IF NEEDED)
* 1 BANANA
* 8 LARGE STRAWBERRIES (WASHED AND WITH STEMS REMOVED)
* 2 CUPS SPINACH (WASHED)
* BLENDER

1 Combine all ingredients in a blender.

2 Puree until smooth. Add more orange juice if you like a thinner smoothie.

3 Bottoms up! Pour into a glass and enjoy.

TIP: TRY ADDING RASPBERRIES OR BLUEBERRIES FOR A NEW SMOOTHIE FLAVOR!

TIP: ADD ONE TABLESPOON OF HONEY TO THE SMOOTHIE FOR EXTRA SWEETNESS.

PLANT WATERCRESS

Watercress is a salad green that loves to have its roots submerged in water and it only requires a few hours of morning sunlight. We can easily grow this peppery crop indoors for a healthy addition to homemade meals!

YOU WILL NEED:

- A SHALLOW POT OR CONTAINER WITH A TRAY FOR DRAINAGE
- PERLITE
- WATERCRESS CUTTINGS

FACT: PERLITE IS A NATURALLY OCCURRING MINERAL DERIVED FROM VOLCANIC GLASS. IT IS EXCELLENT AT HOLDING WATER! YOU CAN BUY IT FROM MOST GARDENING STORES.

1 Fill a shallow potting dish ½ full with perlite. Saturate the growing mix with water. Make sure the drainage tray is placed underneath the pot to catch any excess water.

3 Place in a shady spot indoors, away from strong afternoon sunlight.

5 Harvest your homegrown watercress by snipping off the tops of the plants with scissors. Try to enjoy their peppery crunch before they flower. If they produce petals/blooms, the flavor will be bitter!

4 Keep the soil very wet, being sure to add water every day if needed.

2 Place the stems of the watercress into the dish and bury them about ¼-inch deep. They will sprout roots within a few days!

BAKE SALTY KALE CHIPS

Kale is one of the many greens that can be planted in early spring and harvested later in the season, or in the summer. When eaten raw, it can be tough and hard to chew, but if you season the leaves with salt and bake them in the oven, kale becomes a crunchy tasty snack!

YOU WILL NEED:

- 1 BUNCH OF KALE (WASHED, DRIED, WITH STEMS REMOVED)
- 1 TABLESPOON OLIVE OIL
- SALT AND PEPPER TO TASTE
- BAKING SHEET
- GREASEPROOF PAPER

1 Preheat the oven to 350°F. Tear the kale leaves into small pieces. Kale stems and any blemished leaves can be composted.

2 Place the torn kale leaves onto a baking sheet lined with greaseproof paper.

3 Drizzle the kale with the olive oil and massage with your hands to ensure it is coated evenly. Season with salt and pepper to taste.

4 Bake the kale for 6 minutes. With a grown-up's help, carefully remove the baking sheet and flip the leaves. Then bake for another 5 minutes.

5 Remove the kale chips. The edges should be crunchy. Bake a little longer, if needed. Once ready, allow them to cool slightly before digging in!

TIP: BE SURE TO FULLY DRY THE KALE LEAVES AFTER WASHING. ANY MOISTURE WILL CAUSE THE KALE CHIPS TO BE MUSHY INSTEAD OF CRISP!

TIP: FOR A FLAVOR TWIST, ADD 1 TEASPOON OF CUMIN, GARLIC, OR SMOKED PAPRIKA DURING STEP 3.

LILAC

Lilacs are a late-spring flower. Their fragrance is strong and they attract butterflies.

CROCUS

Crocus flowers emerge early in the season. They grow from a bulb.

PEONY

Peonies mark the end of spring flower season and the beginning of summer.

SNOWDROPS

Snowdrops are one of the first flowers to bloom, often when there is still snow on the ground.

SPRING FLOWERS

After the long winter, spring is a time of color and excitement. Green sprouts emerge from the cold soil and farmers and gardeners watch closely for the first flowers to bud and bloom. Soon it will be time to plant fruits and vegetables! Some flowers grow best in the long days of summer, but many prefer the cooler temperatures and nourishing rainfall of spring. Let's look at a few common flower varieties.

HELLEBORE

Hellebores bloom in late winter and early spring—even when there's still snow! They are one of the first sources of nectar for bees after the long winter.

TULIPS

Tulips are loved by bees. They come in bright colors and have a beautiful cup-like shape.

DAFFODILS

Daffodils can be planted in the fall by placing bulbs in the ground. These yellow flowers bloom early in spring and are closely associated with this season.

HOW TO PRESS FLOWERS

The beauty of fresh flowers doesn't have to fade. Preserve them to enjoy for years to come by pressing the delicate blooms between the pages of a book. You can then display these blossoms in frames, or use them in crafts—such as homemade cards for springtime holidays like Mother's Day! Discover how …

YOU WILL NEED:

- FRESH FLOWERS
- SCISSORS
- PARCHMENT PAPER
- A HEAVY BOOK
- CARD PAPER (OPTIONAL)
- WHITE GLUE (OPTIONAL)

1 Gather fresh flowers on a sunny day. Make sure they're dry, not covered in rain or dew.

2 If you only want the blossoms, cut off the stem at the base of the flower heads. Or, you can press the flowers with the stems intact, too.

3 Place the flowers between a folded sheet of parchment paper (or between two sheets).

4 Insert the parchment paper with the flowers inside, between the pages of a heavy book.

5 Close the book and weight it down with extra books on top. Leave the flowers inside for 1 week.

6 If they are not fully dry and flat, leave inside the book to press longer, for up to 4 weeks.

To use the finished pressed flowers in a homemade card, simply create a card by folding a sheet of card paper in half. Write a special message inside, then stick the pressed flowers to the front of the card with a dab of white glue. You can use markers or crayons to decorate around the flowers, too.

EDIBLE FLOWERS

Did you know there are some flowers that you can safely harvest and eat? It's true! We can add these beautiful blossoms to drinks, baked goods, and other recipes. Be sure to always research which flowers are safe and which ones are toxic before eating any blossoms. Never harvest any flowers that are rotting, dirty, blemished, or may have been chemically treated.

ROSE (PETALS)
We can use clean, blemish-free rose petals to add flavor and color to jams, sauces, cakes, and more.

CHAMOMILE
Chamomile flowers have a fresh-apple scent and, when steeped in hot water for tea, can be very calming and relaxing.

PANSY
Pansies are said to have a lettuce-like flavor with a touch of sweetness. Their bold colors make beautiful and edible decorations to home-baked cakes.

SQUASH BLOSSOM

Available in late spring or early summer, the bright yellow or orange flowers of squash and gourd plants are slightly sweet.

LAVENDER

The blossoms of lavender taste sweet and flowery. These blooms are scrumptious in baked goods and sweets.

NASTURTIUM

With its peppery flavor, nasturtium blooms are a tasty addition to savory salads.

ELDERFLOWER

Blossoms from elderberry plants are safe to consume and can be harvested in late spring. Add elderflowers to lemonade for a delicious twist! NOTE: never eat raw elderberries.

CALENDULA (PETALS)

A member of the marigold family, calendula petals are delicious sprinkled on salads. When sautéed in oil, folks say they taste like saffron!

WONDERFUL WEEDS

Weeds are flowers and plants that grow without our help. Some weeds grow by spreading their roots far and wide under the soil. Others spread their seeds through the wind, or with help from wild animals. Some weeds are considered a nuisance and some are poisonous. But there are many weeds that are helpful, beautiful, contain medicinal properties, and are edible. You probably have a few of these plants growing right outside your doorstep!

COMMON VIOLETS

Violets are very strong little plants! They have special stems, called rhizomes, that grow horizontally underground and develop roots and shoots that turn into new violet plants. Violets also spread by shooting seeds into the air; sometimes up to 3 or 4 feet! The flowers and the leaves of blue and white violets are edible. Yellow violets should be avoided.

- VIOLET BLOSSOMS CAN BE USED TO MAKE VINEGAR.
- IT IS SAID THAT VIOLET LEAVES HELP REDUCE SWELLING WHEN PLACED ON INJURIES OR WOUNDS.
- VIOLET FLOWERS CAN BE COATED IN SUGAR AND EATEN LIKE CANDY.

DANDELIONS

Have you ever seen a fuzzy, white dandelion and blown on it to make a wish? The seeds are spread by the wind in the same way. Once the seed meets the ground, dandelions create a long taproot to anchor themselves. The root, leaves, stem, and blossom are all edible.

- DANDELION GREENS ARE VERY NUTRITIOUS AND CAN BE ADDED TO SALADS!
- THE ROOT CAN BE DRIED, ROASTED, AND USED TO MAKE A COFFEE-LIKE DRINK.
- BLOSSOMS CAN BE DRIED AND USED FOR TEA AND MEDICINE.

BREW SWEET VIOLET SYRUP

There are lots of uses for backyard wildflowers like violets. The blossoms taste slightly sweet with a hint of pepper and we can use them to make syrup. This syrup is thinner and lighter than typical pancake syrup. It's perfect for drizzling over ice cream, baked goods, or for creating fun drinks like violet lemonade. This recipe makes about three half-pint jars of syrup.

1 Gently pluck the violet petals from the green base of the flower. Discard the base (called the calyx). Place the petals in a heat-safe bowl.

2 With a grown-up's help, bring the water to a boil in a small saucepan.

3 Pour the hot water over the violet petals. Leave to steep for 24 hours.

4 Place the sugar and violet-infused water into a small saucepan. Bring to a simmer and stir until the sugar is dissolved into a syrup.

5 Strain the syrup into canning jars—using a funnel can be helpful. Discard the petals. Allow the syrup to cool.

6 Once the syrup has cooled, seal the jars and store in the refrigerator for up to 6 weeks.

YOU WILL NEED:

- 1-2 CUPS VIOLET BLOSSOMS
- 1 CUP WATER
- 1 CUP GRANULATED SUGAR
- HEAT-SAFE BOWL
- CANNING JARS
- SAUCEPAN
- STRAINER
- FUNNEL

BAKE EDIBLE FLOWER COOKIES

These sugar cookies aren't just delicious to eat; they are beautiful to look at too! The flavor may vary depending on which flowers you choose to use. For example, cookies topped with nasturtium will taste more savory than lavender cookies. Foraged wild flowers such as violet and dandelion are great, too (see more about edible wildflowers on pages 16–19). This recipe makes about 24–30 cookies.

YOU WILL NEED:

- AN ASSORTMENT OF PRESSED EDIBLE FLOWERS (PRESSED FOR ABOUT 1 HOUR BEFORE BAKING)
- 1/2 CUP POWDERED SUGAR (SIFTED)
- 2 CUPS ALL-PURPOSE FLOUR
- 1 CUP BUTTER (ROOM TEMPERATURE)
- STAND MIXER/HAND-HELD MIXER
- PLASTIC-/BEESWAX-WRAP
- ROLLING PIN
- COOKIE CUTTERS
- BAKING SHEET
- PARCHMENT PAPER

1 Combine the butter and powdered sugar in a large bowl. Mix until well combined and fluffy (about 2 minutes). You can do this by hand with a wooden spoon, too—but it takes a little longer.

2 Add the flour and mix (or stir) just until the ingredients combine.

3 Turn out the dough on a flat work surface dusted with powdered sugar. Form a disc and wrap in plastic- or beeswax-wrap. Chill in the refrigerator for 30 minutes.

4 Remove the dough and roll out on the sugared work surface. It should be no more than ½ an inch thick. Use cookie cutters to create shapes. Place these on a baking sheet lined with parchment paper.

5 Bake at 350°F for 12 minutes or until the edges of the cookies are golden. Remove and immediately press the blossoms onto the tops of the hot cookies, very gently—take care not to burn yourself and be sure to ask a grown-up for help.

6 Leave to cool, then dig in!

MAKE BLOSSOM BATH SALTS

The thaw of the frozen winter soil mixed with spring rainfall creates a lot of mud and muck. In fact, spring is often nicknamed "mud season." … And mud season means more baths! We can make bathtime more fun by making our own bath salts. Using flowers or herbs that are beginning to grow is a fun way to bring the outdoors in during this time of year.

YOU WILL NEED:

- 1 ½ CUPS EPSOM SALT
- ½ CUP PINK HIMALAYAN SEA SALT
- 2 TABLESPOONS BAKING SODA
- HANDFUL OF DRIED LAVENDER BUDS
- HANDFUL OF DRIED CALENDULA BLOSSOMS
- HANDFUL OF DRIED ROSE PETALS
- PINT-SIZED CANNING JAR

TIP: THESE BATH SALTS MAKE A GREAT GIFT FOR MOTHER'S DAY OR FOR MAY BASKETS! SIMPLY ADD A RIBBON AND GIFT TAG TO THE JAR.

1 Combine the salts and baking soda in a mixing bowl. Stir to mix.

2 Add the dried blossoms, petals, and buds. Stir again to combine all ingredients evenly.

3 Carefully pour the contents of the mixing bowl into the jar and secure the lid.

4 At bathtime, add one or two tablespoons of the blossom bath salt mix to warm bath water. Sit back, soak it up, and relax!

DYE EASTER EGGS

Dyeing eggs for the springtime festival of Easter is a fun way to celebrate the season. Did you know you can easily change the color of the egg by using plants and other natural items? Simply use the base recipe below and add the pigment ingredients to create your favorite color. Be sure to ask a grown-up for help when using the hob.

BASE RECIPE:

- HARDBOILED EGGS
- 1 CUP WATER PER PIGMENT RECIPE
- 1 TABLESPOON WHITE VINEGAR PER PIGMENT RECIPE
- PIGMENT INGREDIENTS

PIGMENT RECIPES:

- YELLOW: 2 TABLESPOONS CURRY/TURMERIC POWDER
- PINK/PURPLE: 1 CUP SHREDDED BEETS
- BLUE: 1 CUP CHOPPED PURPLE CABBAGE
- ORANGE: 1 CUP SHALLOT/YELLOW ONION SKINS

1 Choose which color(s) you'd like to make—if making multiple colors use multiple pots. Combine the pigment ingredients and the water in a pot on the stove.

3 Strain the dyed water into a heat-safe bowl. Discard the solid ingredients by composting. Add the vinegar. Allow the solution to cool.

5 When you're happy with the color, remove the eggs from the dye bath with a slotted spoon. Leave to air dry on a piece of paper towel or parchment paper.

4 Place the hardboiled eggs in the dye mixture and soak for several hours or overnight. The longer the eggs soak, the deeper the color will be. Make sure the eggs are fully submerged in the liquid.

6 Finished hardboiled eggs can be stored in the refrigerator, ready to eat. They can also be placed around the home or outdoors for an Easter egg hunt!

2 Warm over medium heat and simmer for 20 minutes to allow the fruit or vegetables to leach their color into the water.

MAKE EASTER EGG CHICKS

After dyeing our Easter eggs, it can be hard to think of ways to use them up.
A fun and tasty way to make sure our dyed Easter eggs don't go to waste
is to create this appetizer—perfect for a spring picnic or party.
A grown-up should help with any cutting or slicing.

YOU WILL NEED:

- 6 HARDBOILED EGGS (COOLED)
- 2 TABLESPOONS MAYONNAISE
- ½ TEASPOON DIJON MUSTARD
- 1 PINCH GARLIC POWDER

- ½ RED OR ORANGE BELL PEPPER (CORED, SEEDED, AND SLICED)
- RAISINS (HALVED)
- PARSLEY

TIP: A NEAT WAY TO REMOVE THE YOLKS IS TO GENTLY SQUEEZE THE BASE OF THE EGGS—THIS PUSHES THE YOLK UP AND OUT!

1 Peel the eggs, then carefully slice off a thin layer from the bottom of each egg—this will allow the eggs to stand up. Next, cut off the top ⅓ of each egg and set the tops aside. (You can discard or eat the bottom slices!)

2 Remove the yolks from the eggs and place the yolks in a bowl—taking care not to break or squish the rest of the eggs. Mash the yolks well with a fork. Add the mayonnaise, mustard, and garlic powder to the bowl and stir to combine all the ingredients.

3 Carefully spoon the yolk filling back into the eggs. Place the top of each egg on top of the filling. Be careful not to push too hard!

4 Take a slice of bell pepper and carefully cut it into small triangles. Use two triangles to create a beak and gently push them into the filling. Next, add raisins to create the eyes. Repeat for all eggs.

5 Carefully place each finished egg onto a serving tray. Garnish with parsley so it looks like the chicks are outdoors!

SPRING CROP: STRAWBERRIES

Strawberries are one of our favorite crops to grow on the homestead. In the spring, small white strawberry blossoms grow. Honeybees and other insects flutter to the blossoms and pollinate them, and the strawberry plants then begin to form berries. When they have grown and are ready for picking, the strawberries turn bright red and have a sweet, fruity fragrance.

There are two groups of strawberries we can grow; ever-bearing varieties and June-bearing varieties.

JUNE-BEARING

June-bearing varieties fruit early in the summer and not again until the following year.

EVER-BEARING

Ever-bearing varieties produce blossoms and fruit all spring through summer.

Strawberries are unusual plants because when they are ready to reproduce, they send out side-shoots from the main "mother plant." These shoots, called runners or "stolons," root themselves into the soil and a new clone plant is created. The new plant is called a daughter. After the daughter is rooted and growing, the runners dry and shrivel away.

GROW BARE-ROOT STRAWBERRIES

Planting your own strawberries is easy. Simply purchase bare-root plants from a garden center or store and follow the steps below. If you plant your strawberry plants in early spring, you should have your first fruits by late spring and into the summer!

YOU WILL NEED:

- 3-4 BARE-ROOT STRAWBERRY PLANTS
- LARGE FLOWERPOT WITH A DRAINAGE TRAY
- POTTING SOIL
- TROWEL

FACT:

A BARE-ROOT STRAWBERRY PLANT IS SOLD AS A SET OF ROOTS WITHOUT SOIL—WHEN IN THIS STATE, THE PLANT IS DORMANT, WHICH IS KIND OF LIKE BEING ASLEEP! WHEN THE PLANT IS WATERED AND BURIED IN SOIL, IT WILL WAKE UP AND BEGIN TO GROW.

1 Soak the roots in water for at least 20 minutes to hydrate.

2 Fill the flowerpot with potting soil about ¾ full.

3 Gently open the roots, and fan them outward, away from the center stem.

4 Set the spread-out strawberry plants on the top of the potting soil. Leave about 8 inches of space between each plant.

5 Add a layer of potting soil on top, covering the roots. Keep the stems at soil level, uncovered.

6 Gently sprinkle with water and leave the pot in the sun—these plants need lots of sunlight! Keep the soil evenly moist. New leaves should sprout after 2 to 3 weeks and the fruit will follow.

TIP:

IF YOU HAVE A GARDEN, YOU CAN BUY EVEN MORE BARE-ROOT STRAWBERRY PLANTS AND PLANT THEM DIRECTLY INTO THE SOIL.

MAKE YUMMY STRAWBERRY JAM

After the long winter months, it's so exciting to harvest homegrown berries. A neat way to use fresh springtime fruit is to make jam. Strawberry jam is a delicious treat on homemade bread, crackers, or even in cookies! This recipe makes about four jam jars' worth of jam.

YOU WILL NEED:

- 2 POUNDS FRESH FULLY RIPENED STRAWBERRIES (CLEANED AND WITH STEMS REMOVED)
- 3 TABLESPOONS FRESH LEMON JUICE
- 1 1/3 CUP HONEY
- LARGE POT
- POTATO MASHER
- 4 CLEAN JAM JARS

1 With a grown-up's help, roughly chop the strawberries and place them in a large pot on the stove over medium heat. Add the lemon juice and honey and stir. After about 5 minutes, the strawberries will become mushy. Ask a grown-up to help mash the strawberry pieces over the stove with a potato masher.

3 Continue cooking the jam until it thickens, about 5 minutes more. To test, simply dip a spoon into the jam. If it runs off the spoon like a sauce, it's not ready. It should be thick.

4 Once ready, remove the jam from the heat and leave to cool completely. Finally, spoon into clean glass jars and dig in! You can store leftovers in the refrigerator for up to 2 weeks.

TIP:
IF THE JAM IS TOO THIN AFTER IT HAS COOLED, SIMPLY REHEAT AND SIMMER FOR ANOTHER 5–10 MINUTES. ALLOW TO COOL AND TRY AGAIN.

2 Bring the mashed strawberry mixture to a simmer (it should be gently bubbling) and continue to cook for about 1 hour. Stir often.

ROLL STRAWBERRY FRUIT LEATHERS

Strawberries are delicious when eaten straight from the garden. Sometimes there's so many to harvest that we can't eat them fast enough! Making homemade fruit leathers is a great way to dry the strawberries and keep them onhand for eating later. This recipe makes one large sheet of leathers (about 10 rolls).

YOU WILL NEED:

- 1 POUND FRESH AND FULLY RIPENED STRAWBERRIES (CLEANED AND WITH STEMS REMOVED)
- 1 TABLESPOON LEMON JUICE
- 1 TABLESPOON HONEY (OPTIONAL)
- BLENDER
- BAKING SHEET
- PARCHMENT PAPER

1 Heat the oven to the lowest setting possible.

2 Line a baking sheet with parchment paper.

3 Combine the strawberries, lemon juice, and honey (if using) in a blender. Blend until smooth.

4 Pour out the puree onto the baking sheet. Use a spatula to spread it in an even layer, about ⅛ of an inch thick.

5 Bake for 4–5 hours, or until the surface of the puree is no longer sticky. With a grown-up's help, remove from the oven and allow to cool completely. Don't overbake it, or it will become too stiff.

6 Slice the fruit leather and parchment paper into strips—scissors or a pizza cutter are handy for this.

7 Roll up each strip and enjoy!

TIP: IF THE EDGES ARE CRISP, SIMPLY CUT THEM OFF BEFORE ROLLING THE LEATHER!

TIP: STORE IN AN AIRTIGHT CONTAINER IN THE REFRIGERATOR FOR UP TO 5 DAYS.

CRAFT A FORAGED WIND CHIME

Wind chimes are outdoor decorations that also double up as musical instruments. Objects like small sticks, poles, or shells dangle from a string tied to a larger stick or base. When the wind blows, the objects knock together creating a sound many people find relaxing and soothing. People have made wind chimes for thousands of years! Follow the steps to make your own wind chime by foraging items found throughout nature and hanging them from a stick.

YOU WILL NEED:

- A STURDY STICK, 6 INCHES LONG X ½ INCH IN DIAMETER
- STRING OR YARN
- SCISSORS
- FORAGED ITEMS FROM THE OUTDOORS SUCH AS STICKS, SEASHELLS, AND ROCKS

1 Start by cutting a length of string or yarn (about 12 inches long). Tie one end of the string to one end of your main sturdy branch, then tie the other end of the string to the other end of the branch. You should end up with a long loop—this will be used to hang your wind chime later.

2 Count the number of items you've gathered and would like to hang from your chime. This is the number of extra strings you will cut.

3 Cut the strings roughly the same length, at least 6 inches long.

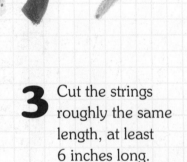
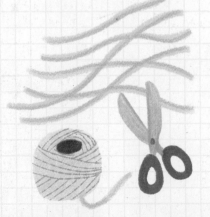

4 Tie one end of each string around the main, large stick. Be sure they are knotted and secure.

5 Tie the opposite end of each string around each object, making sure they are secure.

6 Decide where you'd like to hang your wind chime. How high will it hang? Ask a grown-up to help you hang it. Then sit back and wait for the wind to blow!

TIP:

YOU CAN PAINT YOUR OBJECTS BEFORE YOU STRING THEM UP TO MAKE YOUR WIND CHIME MORE COLORFUL.

MAKE MINI MAY BASKETS

The giving of a May basket on the first day of May is an old tradition. A small, homemade basket was created and filled with flowers, small gifts, and treats. May baskets were secretly left on the doorstep or hung from the doorknob of a friend's home. This ritual celebrates the return of spring and is meant to spread cheer to our friends and loved ones. Learn how to create your own mini May baskets.

YOU WILL NEED:

- PAPER CUPS OR SMALL BUCKETS
- HOLE PUNCH
- RIBBON
- SCISSORS
- ITEMS TO DECORATE YOUR BASKET, SUCH AS MARKER PENS, COLORED PAPER, AND YARN
- ITEMS TO FILL YOUR BASKET (SEE BELOW)

GOODIES TO FILL YOUR BASKET

Try to fill your basket with natural or homemade items, and things that remind you of spring. If herbs or flowers are currently growing outdoors, tying small bundles together with ribbon are a great addition.

You could also fill your basket with the things you've made in this book, including tiny jars of homemade bath salts, violet syrup, flower cookies, or homemade jam!

1 If using a bucket, skip to step 3. If using a paper cup, ask a grown-up to help you use the hole punch. Punch two holes in the cup roughly ½ an inch down from the opening. Holes should be punched on opposite sides from one another.

2 Cut a piece of ribbon at least 8 inches long. Tie one end of the ribbon through one hole and secure with a knot on the inside of the cup. Repeat on the other side. This is your basket and handle!

3 Decorate the outside of the basket with markers, paper, ribbons, yarn, pressed flowers—whatever you like!

4 Fill the basket carefully with homemade goodies and flowers or herbs.

5 Take your finished May basket to your friend's doorstep. Be very quiet and sneaky! Leave it in front of the doorway for them to find and spread the spring cheer.

Brimming with creative inspiration, how-to projects, and useful information to enrich your everyday life, quarto.com is a favorite destination for those pursuing their interests and passions.

Inspiring | Educating | Creating | Entertaining

First published in 2022 by Ivy Kids, an imprint of The Quarto Group.
100 Cummings Center, Suite 265D, Beverly, MA 01915, USA.
T +1 978-282-9590 F +1 078-283-2742 www.QuartoKnows.com

A CIP record for this book is available from the Library of Congress.

ISBN 978-0-7112-7283-5
eISBN 978-0-7112-7282-8

The illustrations were created with color pencils
Set in ITC Souvenir, Cream, Cantoria, Palmer Lake, Wisely

Published by Georgia Amson-Bradshaw • Edited by Hannah Dove
Designed by Sasha Moxon • Production by Dawn Cameron

Manufactured in the USA by Jostens on recycled FSC® paper, JO012022

9 8 7 6 5 4 3 2 1

RECYCLED
Paper made from recycled material
FSC
www.fsc.org FSC® C103061